It was a sunny day in Thornfizzle, Ohio, and the last day of the school year. A shiny red bicycle sped down a tree lined sidewalk. Riding on the bicycle was a smiling young boy named Scotty. He slowed down and stopped in front of a two story house with a big porch and green shutters.

6446

Scotty got off his bike and walked up the sidewalk to the porch. He noticed an envelope sticking out of the mailbox. He took it out and started to grin. Scotty threw open the screen door and hollered.

& Scotty
fizzle, OH
12345

"Hey Mom!
A voice echoed from the hallway. "What's all the commotion, young man?"

"Uncle Billy and Auntie Dee sent us a letter. Can I open it?"

"Well," his mom said, "It's addressed to all of us. Yes, you can open it, Scotty."

"Thanks Mom," said Scotty as he took the envelope.

He opened the letter and began to read. His eyes began to glow.

"They want me to come and help at their carnival this summer," said Scotty. "Please, can I, Mom?"

Scotty heard footsteps. He turned around and saw his dad.

"Dad, guess what? Uncle Billy and Auntie Dee want me to help at the carnival this summer. Can I, please?"

Scotty's dad scratched his chin for a moment.

"Hum," he mumbled. "If it's okay with your mom, it's okay with me."

Scotty turned and looked at his mother. Mom smiled and said, "You've done so well in school this year – you deserve a reward. Pack your bags. You're going to the carnival for the summer." Scotty jumped for joy, then ran upstairs to pack.

The next morning Scotty and his parents drove to the train station. They all hugged and said goodbye. As Scotty was boarding the train, his mom shouted, "Uncle Billy and Auntie Dee will be waiting for you when you get off the train."

"Okay!" shouted back Scotty.

A few hours later the train began to slow. Scotty looked out the window and could see his Uncle Billy and Auntie Dee near the gate. He grabbed his bags and ran off the train. They gave Scotty a big hug and said, "Let's go!"

As they were driving, Uncle Billy talked about some strange things that had been happening.

"I think the carnival is haunted," said Uncle Billy.

"Haunted?" Scotty laughed. "I don't believe in that stuff."

"Yeah," laughed Uncle Billy. "Still, there's some strange things going on."

"Like what?" asked Scotty.

"Last week, Auntie Dee went to our car to get a box she had left in the back seat. She noticed all the tires were flat. When she showed me the car, minutes later, the tires were full again."

"Last night, I put the monkeys in their cage. I went to sleep, but was soon awoken by a loud sound. I ran out and found the monkeys riding on the Ferris Wheel. We also hear scary noises in the middle of the night."

"I'm getting scared, Scotty," said Uncle Billy. "Maybe Auntie Dee and I should sell the carnival to Mr. Greenfinger."

"Who's Mr. Greenfinger?" asked Scotty.

"He's the new manager we hired to help run things around here. He told us if we ever wanted to sell the business, he would buy it."

Scotty, Uncle Billy and Auntie Dee arrived at the carnival. After closing time, Scotty decided to go out for a walk through the carnival. He was thinking what a great place this was.

Suddenly, he noticed a bright glow outside Mr. Greenfinger's trailer. He walked closer and saw an incredible sight. Two glowing figures were looking into the trailer windows.

"Hi," said Scotty.

They turned around and smiled at Scotty.

"Hi, I'm Rochester and this is Merle. We're ghosts on vacation."

"It's nice to meet you, I'm Scotty. What are you guys doing?" he asked.

"We come to this carnival every year to go on all the great rides. But this year there's trouble," said Rochester.

"The new manager, Mr. Greenfinger, is trying to trick your Uncle Billy and Auntie Dee into selling the carnival to him. Look in the window and see for yourself," said Merle. Scotty looked into the window.

Mr. Greenfinger was inside talking to a short clown, two baboons, and the carnival handyman.

"Thank you for helping me scare the owners. They think this place is haunted," snickered Mr. Greenfinger. His guests laughed.

"I think they're about to sell the carnival to me. Soon, this place will be mine and I'll make all the money," Mr. Greenfinger chuckled.

Scotty looked at Rochester and Merle and asked, "What can we do?"
"We'll give Mr. Greenfinger a taste of his own medicine,"
said Rochester.
"Would you like to watch the excitement,
Scotty?" asked Merle.
"Boy, would I," said Scotty.
Scotty stayed
by the window
and watched.

Mr. Greenfinger turned off the lights and hopped into bed. Suddenly, he felt wet sandpaper moving across his face. He jumped up and, turning on the light, found a goat standing next to his bed.

It had been licking his face. Mr. Greenfinger chased the goat out the door.

"This is crazy!" thought Mr. Greenfinger. "I need a drink of water."
He reached for the water cup on the nightstand. He took a drink and spit it out.
"Turnip juice! Who put turnip juice in my water cup?" he shouted, "I hate turnip juice!"

Mr. Greenfinger ran to the kitchen to get a drink of water to wash the taste out of his mouth. He grabbed a towel to wipe the goat slime off. The towel was covered with tar. He smeared it all over his face.

As Mr. Greenfinger walked back to his bed, he slipped on some grease that Rochester had put on the floor. He skidded across the room and slid under his bed.

23

Scratching his head nervously, he got back in bed when suddenly loud music started playing. Mr. Greenfinger jumped up in terror. The radio was blarring. He ran over and turned it off.
"What's going on?" Mr. Greenfinger wondered.
He got back in bed.

"Move over!" said Rochester.

"Yeah, move over!" said Merle.

"Oh, sorry," Mr. Greenfinger politely said. Suddenly, he realized he was talking to ghosts. "Ahhhhhhhhhhhhhhh!" he screamed.

He jumped up and hung on the ceiling fan.
Rochester turned it on, and Mr. Greenfinger started
spinning around faster and faster.

He lost his grip and flew out the window right into a garbage can.

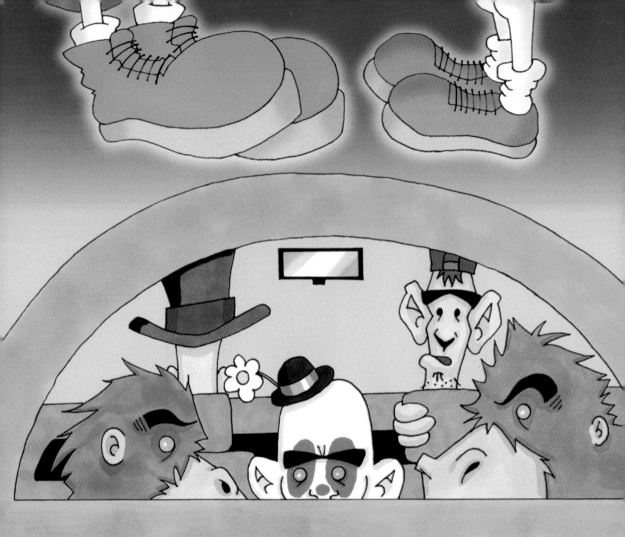

Mr. Greenfinger sped out past his helpers. They turned to see Rochester and Merle coming. They all ran and jumped into Mr. Greenfinger's little car. Mr. Greenfinger turned the key, but it would not start. Rochester and Merle began jumping up and down on the roof.

Everyone was screaming. Mr. Greenfinger tried to roll up his window, but it was stuck. Rochester flew down and pulled Mr. Greenfinger's hat down over his ears. Merle opened the door and sprayed them all with whipped cream.

Finally, the car started and they sped off. Uncle Billy came out to see what was going on. As the car flew by, Mr. Greenfinger and his helpers all yelled,

"WE QUIT!!!"

Uncle Billy saw Rochester and Merle laughing with Scotty.
"Scotty what's going on?" he asked.
"Uncle Billy, meet Rochester and Merle. They're cool ghosts.
Mr. Greenfinger was trying to scare you into selling the carnival.
Rochester and Merle taught them a lesson. It doesn't pay to cheat
and be dishonest. You'll never see him again!" laughed Scotty.

"Thank you for helping us," said Uncle Billy to Rochester and Merle. "You can stay as long as you like."

"Oh boy, that would be great!" said Rochester.

Rochester and Merle stayed all summer playing with Scotty and helping at the carnival.